First U. S. edition 2000

Library of Congress Cataloging-in-Publication Data

Browne, Anthony.
Willy's pictures / Anthony Browne.—1st U.S. ed.
p. cm.
Summary: Willy the chimp paints pictures that are tributes to art masterpieces,
including "American Gothic," "The Birth of Venus," and "Mona Lisa."
ISBN 0-7636-0962-5 (hardcover).—ISBN 0-7636-1323-1 (hardcover library edition)
I. Title.
PZ7.B81984 Wn   2000
[E]—dc21   98-47804

10 9 8 7 6 5 4 3 2 1

Printed in Italy

This book was typeset in Browne; handlettering by Anthony Browne.
The illustrations were done in watercolor and gouache.

Candlewick Press
2067 Massachusetts Avenue
Cambridge, Massachusetts 02140

This book is
dedicated to all
the great artists
who have inspired
me to paint

Look out for
their pictures at
the back of this book

WILLY'S PICTURES

Me   Millie   Buster Nose

Anthony Browne

CANDLEWICK PRESS

CAMBRIDGE, MASSACHUSETTS

Willy likes painting and looking at pictures.
He knows that every picture tells a story . . .

THE BIRTHDAY SUIT

Quick, cover yourself up!

MY BEST EVER SANDCASTLE

I was so pleased with it, but I had an odd feeling
that the castle was trying to warn me of something.

LOTS AND LOTS AND LOTS OF DOTS

We gradually started to notice some
very strange things in the park.

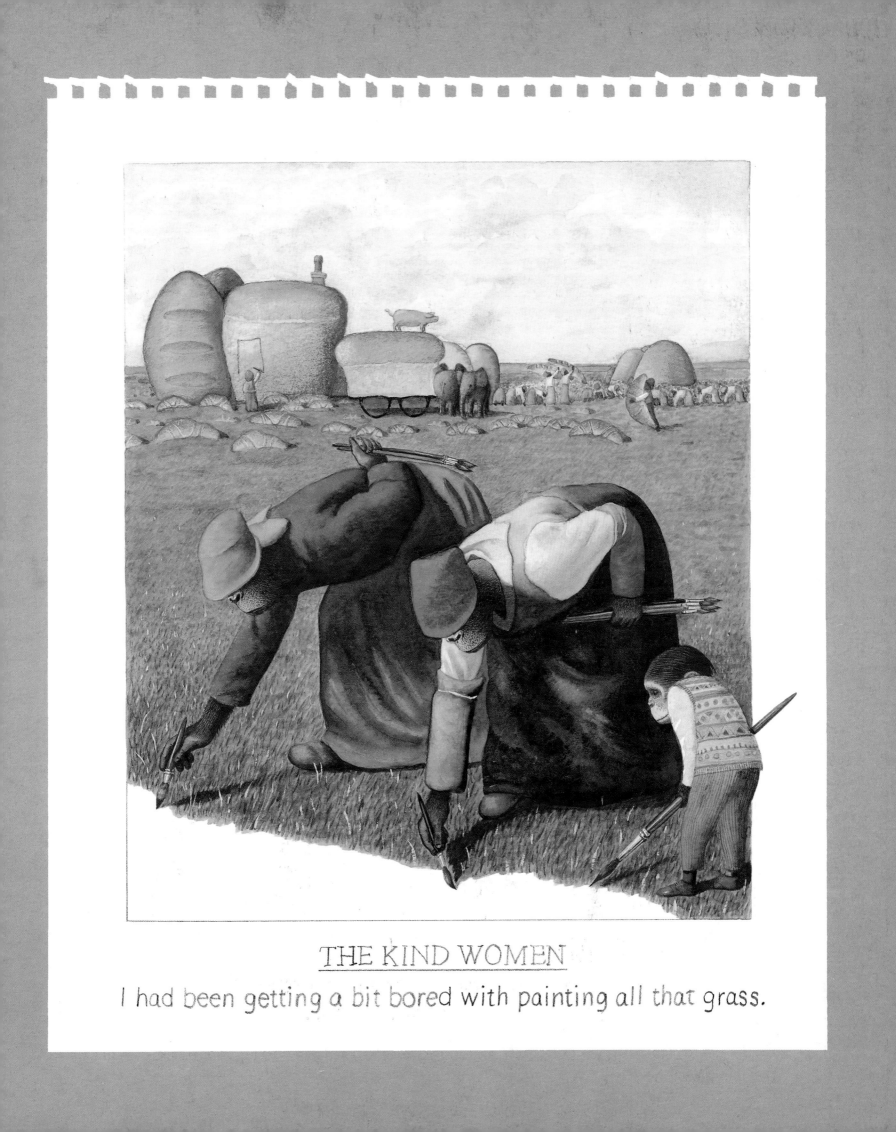

THE KIND WOMEN

I had been getting a bit bored with painting all that grass.

EARLY MORNING DREAM

I'm just taking my dog for a walk . . .

MY BIRTHDAY

At first I thought it was great fun, but would they *ever* stop?

AT THE SWIMMING POOL

Oh no, it's the wrong changing room!

COMING TO LIFE

I was just finishing this painting when I heard
a small voice say, "Give us a hand."

THE MYSTERIOUS SMILE

Can *you* solve the mystery?

THE FRUITFUL FISHING TRIP

We hadn't caught anything all day and were on our
way home when we cast our net for the last time.

ROOM WITHOUT A VIEW

I had always hated looking out of that window,
so one morning I decided to do something about it.

MY NIGHTMARE

The dreadful invitation read, "You are cordially invited to attend the wedding ceremony of Millie and Buster Nose."

AN ODD DAY

As soon as we got there it seemed that Millie was in a hurry to go home. "I'm sorry," she said, "I must fly." And she was off!

LANDSCAPE WITH ONION

We followed it for miles before we finally hunted it down.

NEARLY A SELF-PORTRAIT

Some of my friends wanted to help.

THE HERO

I can dream, can't I?

Now, come for a tour of the
pictures that inspired Willy.
These pictures tell stories too.

Try matching them with
Willy's pictures, and
read what Willy
says about them.

THE STRAW MANNEQUIN
painted between 1791–2 by
Francisco Goya

This is one of a group of pictures that Goya painted when he was still a young man. Although they are just playing a game, it looks a little frightening to me.

SELF-PORTRAIT WITH MONKEYS
painted in 1943 by
Frida Kahlo

Frida Kahlo's paintings are often of herself and her own experiences—she had a difficult life. I like the way she seems to be showing a similarity between herself and the monkeys in this painting.

EARLY SUNDAY MORNING
painted in 1930 by
Edward Hopper

What I like about this picture is the feeling of time standing still, and how a very ordinary scene can seem so extraordinary. It feels just like a Sunday morning to me. Does it to you?

THE HERRING NET
painted in 1885 by
Winslow Homer

During a two-year stay in an English fishing village, Winslow Homer fell in love with the sea and spent the rest of his life painting it. I like this picture because it shows what it must feel like to be out on the cold, wild water. It makes these ordinary fishermen look like heroes.

DAPHNE AND APOLLO
painted between about 1470–80 by
Antonio Pollaiuolo

As well as being a painter, Pollaiuolo was a sculptor and a goldsmith. He lived and worked in Florence. This painting shows the Greek god Apollo chasing after a nymph, Daphne. She prays to be rescued and is turned into a laurel tree. It is one of the funniest, strangest pictures I've ever seen.

THE PAINTER IN HIS STUDIO
painted between 1665–6 by
Jan Vermeer

Jan Vermeer's pictures have a wonderful feeling of space, and subtle effects of light. This is a painting of a painter painting a painting.

THE TOWER OF BABEL
painted in 1563 by
Pieter Brueghel the Elder

This picture is a scene from a story in the Bible. The people of Babylon tried to build a great city with a tower high enough to reach the heavens. God punished them for their pride by causing them to speak different languages and then scattering them across the earth. In this picture, the tower has been abandoned and the babbling Babylonians are scurrying about like ants.

SAINT GEORGE AND THE DRAGON
painted in about 1506 by
Raphael

In this painting, Saint George is saving the king's daughter by slaying the dragon who terrorized the city. Raphael painted more than one picture of Saint George being brave. Perhaps he wanted to be a hero too? (I know I do!)

Sometimes just a tiny part of the original painting shows up in Willy's work, so look carefully!

PARIS, A RAINY DAY
painted between 1876–7 by
Gustave Caillebotte

Caillebotte was very interested in the effects of light. This picture captures the atmosphere of rainy streets; I feel soggy just looking at it.

SELF-PORTRAIT AS ZEUXIS
painted in 1685 by
Aert de Gelder

This picture shows Aert de Gelder dressed a[s] a Greek painter called Zeuxis, who died laughi[ng] while he was painting a funny-looking old woma[n]

LE DÉJEUNER SUR L'HERBE
painted in 1863 by
Edouard Manet

Edouard Manet wanted to be treated as a serious painter, but many people were shocked by this painting and laughed at his work.

THE DOG
painted between 1821–3 by
Francisco Goya

Goya was the court painter for the Spanish royal family. As he grew older he painted many fantastical and frightening pictures. I love the expression on the dog's face.

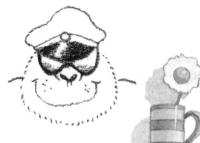

MIDDAY
painted in 1821 by
Caspar David Friedrich

Caspar David Friedrich's pictures are full of "symbols," or meanings. Here, the path the woman is walking along is a symbol of the path of life.

GLAD DAY
painted in 1794 by
William Blake

Blake was a poet as well as a painter. He believed that imagination and the spiritual world were very important. I like the energy and the joy shining from the man in this painting. It makes me feel very glad!

THE MONKEYS
painted in 1906 by
Henri Rousseau

Henri Rousseau didn't start painting until he was forty. He taught himself. He created many simple, dreamy pictures like this one.

STILL LIFE:
VASE WITH TWELVE SUNFLOWERS
painted in 1888 by
Vincent van Gogh

Vincent van Gogh saw beauty in simple, natural things. His pictures were not popular when he painted them, though today they are famous.

Acknowledgments

The author and publisher gratefully acknowledge permission to reproduce the following:

The Arnolfini Marriage, 1434
(oil on panel)
by **Jan van Eyck** (c.1390–1441).
National Gallery, London, UK/Bridgeman Art Library.

The Birth of Venus, c.1485
(tempera on canvas)
by **Sandro Botticelli** (1444/5–1510).
Galleria degli Uffizi, Florence, Italy/Bridgeman Art Library.

Blind Orion Searching for the Rising Sun, 1658 (oil on canvas)
by **Nicolas Poussin** (1594–1665).
The Metropolitan Museum of Art, New York, USA, Fletcher Fund, 1924. (24.45.1). Photograph copyright © 1992 The Metropolitan Museum of Art.

The Creation of Adam: Sistine Chapel Ceiling, 1508–12 (fresco) (post-restoration)
by **Michelangelo Buonarroti** (1475–1564).
Vatican Museums and Galleries, Rome, Italy/Bridgeman Art Library.

Daphne and Apollo, c. 1470–80
by **Antonio Pollaiuolo** (1432/3–98).
National Gallery, London, UK/Bridgeman Art Library.

Le Déjeuner sur l'Herbe, 1863
by **Edouard Manet** (1832–83).
Musée d'Orsay, Paris, France/Bridgeman Art Library.

The Dog, 1821–23
by **Francisco José de Goya y Lucientes** (1746–1828).
Prado, Madrid, Spain/Bridgeman Art Library.

Early Sunday Morning, 1930
(oil on canvas)
by **Edward Hopper** (1882–1967).
Collection of Whitney Museum of American Art, New York, USA. Purchase, with funds from Gertrude Vanderbilt Whitney 31.426. Photograph copyright © 1998 Whitney Museum of American Art.

Glad Day or *The Dance of Albion,* 1794
by **William Blake** (1757–1827).
British Museum, London, UK/Bridgeman Art Library.

The Gleaners, 1857 (oil on canvas)
by **Jean François Millet** (1814–75).
Musée d'Orsay, Paris, France/Bulloz/Bridgeman Art Library.

The Herring Net, 1885
(oil on canvas)
by **Winslow Homer** American (1836–1910).
Mr. and Mrs. Martin A. Ryerson Collection, 1937.1039. Photograph copyright © 1999 The Art Institute of Chicago. All rights reserved.

Midday, 1821
by **Caspar David Friedrich** (1774–1840).
Niedersächsisches Landesmuseum, Hannover, Germany.

Mona Lisa, c.1503–06 (panel)
by **Leonardo da Vinci** (1452–1519).
Louvre, Paris, France/Bridgeman Art Library.

The Monkeys, 1906
by **Henri Julien Rousseau** (1844–1910).
Philadelphia Museum of Art, Pennsylvania, USA/Bridgeman Art Library.

The Painter in His Studio, 1665–66
by **Jan Vermeer** (1632–75).
Kunsthistorisches Museum, Vienna, Austria/Bridgeman Art Library.

Paris, a Rainy Day, 1876–77
by **Gustave Caillebotte** (1848–94).
Musée Marmottan, Paris, France/Peter Willi/Bridgeman Art Library.

Saint George and the Dragon, c.1506
(oil on panel)
by **Raphael** (Raffaello Sanzio) (1483–1520).
Andrew W. Mellon Collection, copyright © 1999 Board of Trustees, National Gallery of Art, Washington, USA (1937.1.26. (26)/PA). Photograph copyright © Board of Trustees, National Gallery of Art, Washington.

Self-portrait as Zeuxis, 1685
by **Aert de Gelder** (1645–1727).
Painting owned by Städelsches Kunstinstitut, Frankfurt, Germany. Photograph by Ursula Edelmann, Frankfurt.

Self-portrait with Monkeys, 1943
by **Frida Kahlo** (1907–54).
Copyright © 1999 Fiduciario Av. 5 de Mayo No. 2, Col. Centro 06059, México, D.F. Reproducción autorizada por el Banco de México. Fiduciario en el Fideicomiso relativo a los Museos Diego Rivera y Frida Kahlo. Reproducción autorizada por el Instituto Nacional de Bellas Artes y Literatura. Photographic material supplied by the Centro Nacional de las Artes, Biblioteca de las Artes (México).

Still Life: Vase with Twelve Sunflowers, 1888
by **Vincent van Gogh** (1853–90).
Neue Pinakothek, Munich, Germany/Giraudon/Bridgeman Art Library.

The Straw Mannequin (El Pelele), 1791–92
by **Francisco José de Goya y Lucientes** (1746–1828).
Prado, Madrid, Spain/Bridgeman Art Library.

Sunday Afternoon on the Island of La Grande Jatte, 1884–86
by **Georges Pierre Seurat** (1859–91).
Art Institute of Chicago, USA/Bridgeman Art Library.

The Tower of Babel, 1563
by **Pieter Brueghel the Elder** (c. 1520–69).
Kunsthistoriches Museum, Vienna, Austria/Bridgeman Art Library.

The Turkish Bath, 1862
by **Jean Auguste Dominique Ingres** (1780–1867).
Louvre, Paris, France/Giraudon/Bridgeman Art Library.

THE ARNOLFINI MARRIAGE
painted in 1434 by
Jan van Eyck

Jan van Eyck could
make his pictures seem
very real because of the way
he painted detail and light and
shade. Everything looks so solid.
I almost feel as though I'm in
the same room as these
two people.

THE CREATION OF ADAM
painted between 1508–12 by
Michelangelo Buonarroti

This is only a small detail from a huge
picture that took Michelangelo four
years to paint — lying flat on his back,
high up on scaffolding. It must have
been lonely, exhausting work. I'm
amazed that just one man created
such a magnificent piece of art.

**BLIND ORION SEARCHING FOR THE
RISING SUN**
painted in 1658 by
Nicolas Poussin

Nicolas Poussin was French but spent much
of his life in Italy. This painting is based on
a classical myth. The giant Orion is seeking
the sun to cure his blindness. I like the
casual way the goddess Diana is leaning
against a cloud.

THE BIRTH OF VENUS
painted in about 1485 by
Sandro Botticelli

This painting is the goddess of love
coming out of the sea and being blown
to the shore by the wind gods. I think it's
the most graceful painting I've ever seen.

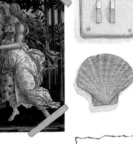

MONA LISA
painted between
about 1503–6 by
Leonardo da Vinci

Leonardo da Vinci's famous
portrait of an unknown
woman must have been one
of his favorites — he took it
everywhere with him.
She has a very mysterious
smile. What do you think
she's smiling about?

THE TURKISH BATH
painted in 1862 by
**Jean Auguste
Dominique Ingres**

Ingres was in his eighties when he
painted this, and he had never been
to Turkey. I love the feeling of the
hot, steaming air in the painting.
I can almost smell the exotic
perfumes.

**SUNDAY AFTERNOON ON THE
ISLAND OF LA GRANDE JATTE**
painted between 1884–6 by
Georges Seurat

When this picture was first shown, people
were shocked by its new technique.
The painting is made from lots of tiny dots
of pure color. I love the way it seems
to shimmer. You have to stand back to
see it properly.

THE GLEANERS
painted in 1857 by
Jean François Millet

Jean François Millet painted peasant life
as it really was — hard work. Here, three poor
women collect the scant remains of the
harvest after it has been reaped; the rich
are far off in the background. I find
it beautiful because it is so plain.